In our last adventure, best friends Amir and Neena were magically pulled into the "Land of the Spirit" by a mysterious amulet. With the help of a wily fox spirit, they quickly learned they now have an important mission: balance this new realm or become stuck there...forever! They healed the mighty Root the Brave by helping him face his fears, but they were thrown right into their next challenge. Will our friends be able to save the day once again, or will this challenge be too great?

www.mascotbooks.com

Carefree, Like Me!: Chapter 2: Sacra the Joyous

For more information, please contact:
Mascot Books
620 Herndon Parkway #320
Herndon, VA 20170
info@mascotbooks.com

Library of Congress Control Number: 2018910754

CPSIA Code: PRT0119A
ISBN-13: 978-1-64307-249-4

Printed in the United States

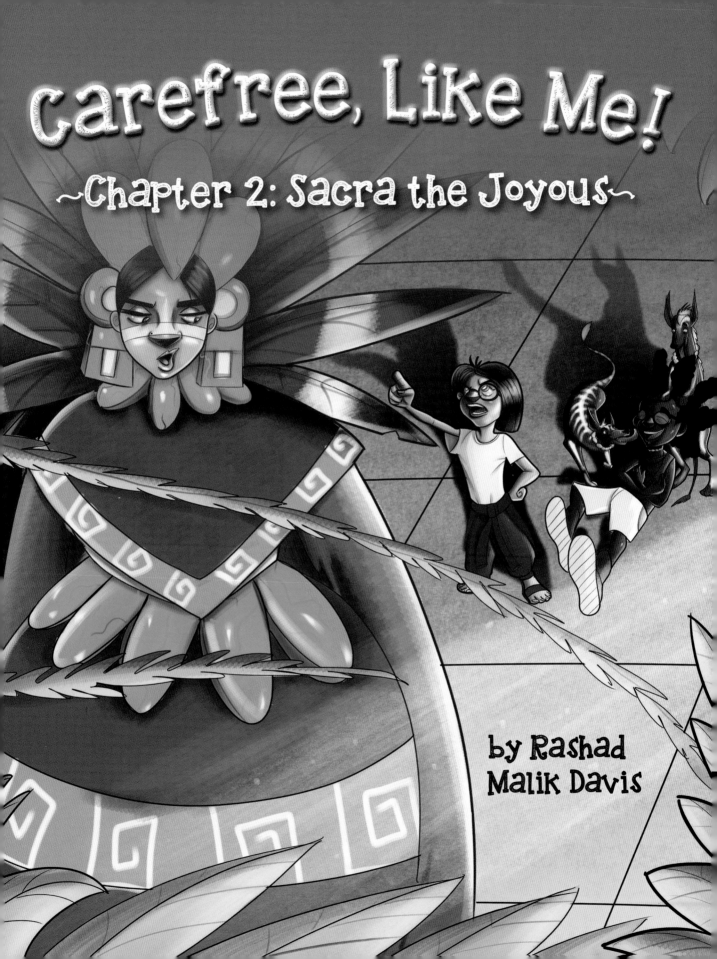

The creature with eyes like diamonds appeared again with a
POOF,
Floating in the air and grinning like a goof.

"You freed King Root! The first deed is complete,
But my dear friends, are you fearless enough for this next feat?

"She sits in the clouds and gives them what they please,
But the land has become dry without even a breeze.
Help to restore the water, grass, fruit, and trees.
Can you help Sacra find the joy she needs?"

"I'm your spirit guide, your friend through and through.
Just trust me and know that you can do it, you two!
Oh, and before I forget: you can call me Ritu!"

Their mysterious guide left with a PUFF,
Leaving Neena and Amir to cough and huff.
The sun was hot. The land was burnt and dry.
The birds were so hot they forgot how to circle in the sky!

"Neena, look! There's smoke coming from over there!
There must be someone. This whole place can't be bare!"
They walked for what seemed like years and days,
Everything melting and dripping in the sun's rays.

The best friends were shocked and amazed by the sight!
Finally, there was an end to their plight!

They shouted and raced to the city walls,
But when they arrived, their hearts did fall.
The city was once humongous and grand,
But now it was ruins covered in dust, rocks, and sand.

Heartbroken, they wandered the streets
looking for someone to speak,
But everyone inside was just too weak!
The people were too hungry, too
thirsty, and too tired to boot,
But from the distance, they could
hear the sound of a flute.

Amir said, "Who's playing that music? Maybe they can help us out.
Maybe they have some water, or a way out of this drought!"
They followed the music through city streets,
looking for the melody that sounded so sweet.

They finally found the musician playing to the sky,
His flute making the sweetest lullaby.
His feet stomped and his feathers whirled.
He spun, jumped, ran, and then twirled.

Amir shouted, "Your music is beautiful, and I don't
mean to interrupt,
But my sweat is getting itchy, and this sun is burning my butt."

He stopped his music and looked at Amir,
Then laughed a deep belly laugh and grinned ear to ear.
"You've come to help like the others before you!
You're chosen to help restore this land to green and blue!"

Neena chimed in, "Who are you? What happened to this place?
Why are there no plants or water? Not even a trace!"

"My name is Ichtaka and I dance to make the rains come,
But our goddess Sacra won't come down from the clouds
and sun!

I've tried everything! I've made offerings of sweet chocolate,
bright jade, and juicy fruit!
Our cacti even got fed up and left from their roots!

I've sung whole songs
backwards while
hopping on one leg.
I've even given her rare,
gold peacock eggs!"

"I would try to fly, but I'm too weak.
I only have enough strength left to speak.
I'm so afraid nothing will make her come down.
This might be the last of our once-majestic town."

Neena shouted, "Why is everyone so doom and gloom?
Neena and Amir are here. Nothing can stop us two!
If she won't come down, we'll just go up!
Soon we'll all be drinking from her royal cup."

Ichtaka smiled, "Make your way up the palace steps.
And take this bit of water, the last I have left.
Don't stop until you've reached the clouds.
Now get up there and make us all proud."

Amir and Neena looked up the temple steps to the sky,
Far past where even the birds would fly.
They climbed until they could climb no more.
They pushed until their legs and feet were sore.

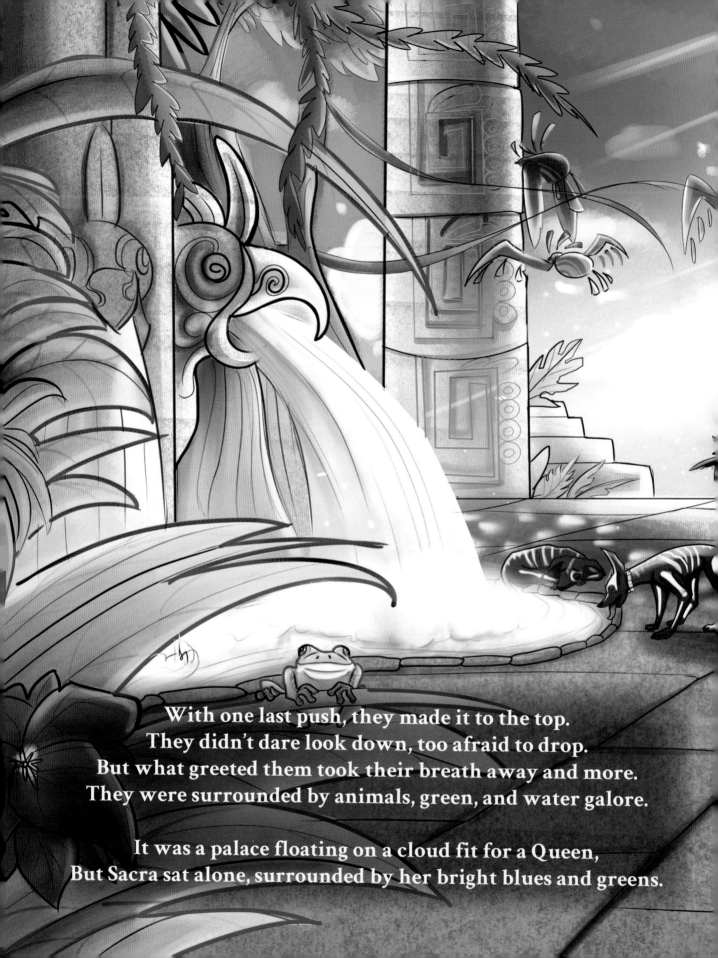

With one last push, they made it to the top.
They didn't dare look down, too afraid to drop.
But what greeted them took their breath away and more.
They were surrounded by animals, green, and water galore.

It was a palace floating on a cloud fit for a Queen,
But Sacra sat alone, surrounded by her bright blues and greens.

Her big voice echoed, "Go away! I want to be left alone!
Leave now, and begone from my throne!"

Neena yelled, "Sacra, how can you leave your people
thirsty and weak?
They're looking for you right now as we speak!
You sit in this room all alone and blue,
But you've got some really important things to do!"

"I can't find my smile! I don't know where it went.
Lately, I've just felt so bored and so spent.
I used to create the winds, flowers, fruit, and corn,
But I've lost my magic. I've just felt so worn."

Amir jumped in, "Well, I've got a trick or two to make you smile!
Just sit back, my lady. Get ready to laugh and go wild!"
He made the silliest face he could and Neena joined in,
But their best faces could barely make Sacra grin.

He grabbed a pie and tossed it at Neena's face,
But it was still so quiet you could hear crickets in the place.

He had to pull out the big guns.
Sacra was a tough crowd,
But Amir just knew he would make this city proud!

He grabbed some fruits and juggled as he walked back,
But he didn't see the edge of the palace, or that the floor had a crack.
He suddenly tumbled, then tripped and fell off the cloud.
He didn't have time to yell or shout. He was heading straight
for the ground!

All hope seemed lost, but Neena jumped for her friend!
That's not how this heroic story would end.
She grabbed Amir and pulled him up with all of her might,
And once he was safe, he kissed and hugged her tight.

Sacra's booming voice came with a grin.
"Neena, you jumped with no doubts to save
your friend's skin.
I was all alone in this tower! I was just a
single soul.
I see all I needed was a friend to help me
know I was whole."

Neena smiled. "You help everyone else in this
land of orange and blue,
But sometimes even a goddess needs a good
friend too!"

They climbed on her back, and she soared into the sky.
She opened her wings wide, and warm rain poured
from the clouds up high.

They made it to the ground, where everyone was dancing in
the water and mud.
The land had grown back, and the canals began to flood!
Sacra smiled and gave them her thanks,
Covering them with her warm and feathery embrace.

Sacra and her new friends cheered and shouted them on,
as the necklace pulled them into a new world and a new dawn.

...The amulet pulled them into a land that was black as night.
They fell into this new place, a hole with no light.
A pair of yellow eyes snapped open in the dark and their fear
grew and grew.
It spoke from the shadows and said, "I've been waiting for
you two..."

Emotional Literacy & Story Comprehension

- There are many normal and healthy emotions we all share. Some of them are anger, love, joy, sadness, and fear. Which of these emotions do you think this book is about?

- In the story, Sacra felt sad because she felt alone. How would you have tried to help Sacra?

- What helps you when you're feeling blue?

- Everyone is different! When you're feeling down, does it help more to talk about it, or do you need alone time? Why?

- Sometimes, sadness doesn't look like someone crying. What are some other ways you can tell if someone is sad or even if you're feeling sad?

Sources Used

Carrasco, David, and Scott Sessions. *Daily Life of the Aztecs.* Greenwood, 2011.

Cooke, Tim. *National Geographic Investigates Ancient Aztec: Archaeology Unlock the Secrets of Mexicos Past.* National Geographic, 2007.

Kenney, Karen Latchana. *Ancient Aztecs.* Essential Library, 2015.

Lourie, Peter. *Hidden World of the Aztec.* Boyds Mills Press, 2006.

Did You Know...

- Sacra's kingdom and her people are based on the Native American Aztec civilization! The Aztec didn't call themselves "Aztec," though. One of the names they called themselves was the Mexica (Meh-she-ka), which is believed to be where we get the name for modern-day Mexico.

- The Mexica lived in modern-day Central Mexico, and its capital city Tenochtitlan (te-nawch-tee-tlahn), is located right beneath the modern-day capital, Mexico City.

- The Mexica spoke Nahuatl (nä-ˌwä-t), a language that's still spoken throughout Central America by the Mexica's descendants and other native Central Americans they encountered as well.

- We can thank the Mexica for some of Mexico's most delicious and famous dishes. They enjoyed, among many other things, tacos, tamales, and tortillas. They filled them with a lot of ingredients, including: vegetables, seafood, turkey, fruits, and insects like grasshoppers.

- The Mexica invented an incredible farming method called the chinampa system. They were called the "floating gardens" by the Spanish, because they were big and fertile mounds of soil floating in water that grew their main crops like corn, beans, tomatoes, chili, and squash.

List of *Carefree, Like Me!* Backers

Adrian	Eugene	LACE	Samantha
Alex O.	Fred	Lauren	Sandhya
Alex W.	Ghali	Louis	Sarah
Alexi	Gianni	Lura	Sasha
Amira	Indigo	Manal	Sebastian
Amy	Isaiah	Marian	Seth
Amsie	Jamasia	Mark	Shira
Angelica	James F.	Matt	Stephanie
Anthony	James K.	Maureen	Talia
Auhmoob	Jay	Maya	Tamara
Barbara	Jennifer Ch.	Molly	Taurean
Bethany	Jennifer Co.	Natalie	The Creative Fund
Bianka	Jeselin	Nicole	Tibby
Brenda	Jill	Nina	Tory & Curtis
Cara	Joanna	Olamide	Unknown
Casseia	Joe	Olive & Michael	Veronica
Cassie	Johnny	Oluwatoni	Virginia
Chen	Justin	Owen	Weke
Christopher	Kashima	Pace Charter School	Whitney
Daniel	Kate	Paris	Wirghoti
Dave D.	Kathleen	PrintNinja	Yinyamina
David J.	Katie	Raymoon	
David C.	Katrina	Robert	
Deborah	Kayla	Rodney	
Eartha	Kenia	Ron	
Emily	Kennedy	Ronke	
Erica	Kimberly	Sam	